THE CHRISTMAS TAIL OF
SAMPSON
THE SILLY-LOOKING SOCK MONKEY

WRITTEN BY SCOTT AND CHRYSTI BURROUGHS · ILLUSTRATED BY SCOTT BURROUGHS

DEDICATED TO **PASTOR TIM WILDER**.
SPECIAL THANKS TO ALL OUR FRIENDS AND FELLOW ARTISTS
AT THE WALT DISNEY FEATURE ANIMATION STUDIO IN FLORIDA.

VERY EARLY IN THE MORNING, ON A COLD AND SNOWY CHRISTMAS DAY, SAMPSON SAT HAPPILY UNDER THE CHRISTMAS TREE.

SAMPSON WAS A SOCK MONKEY AND A SILLY-LOOKING ONE AT THAT. WITH ONE **EAR** LARGER THAN THE OTHER AND

WITHOUT A TAIL, HE WAS QUITE A SILLY SIGHT!

BUT SAMPSON LIKED THE WAY HE LOOKED. ON THE INSIDE HE WAS VERY HAPPY, AND HIS HEART WAS FULL OF KINDNESS. SO, LOOKING SILLY ON THE OUTSIDE DIDN'T BOTHER HIM ONE BIT.

SAMPSON THOUGHT, "I'LL BE THE VERY BEST PRESENT THIS CHRISTMAS DAY!"

SAMPSON WAITED PATIENTLY FOR CHRISTMAS TO BEGIN. SUDDENLY, HE HEARD SOMETHING GO

STOMP,
STOMP,
STOMP!

A LARGE STUFFED ANIMAL BY THE NAME OF BABY THE BULLDOG WAS MARCHING OVER TO HIM.

4

BABY BARKED. "HEY, YOU SILLY-LOOKING SOCK MONKEY! I JUST WANT YOU TO KNOW THAT I'M THE BEST TOY HERE!

I'M BIG AND BLUE, AND I CAN WAG MY TAIL, TOO. AND THAT MAKES ME A BETTER PRESENT THAN YOU!"

"WOW!" SAID SAMPSON. "THAT IS A SUPER-LOOKING TAIL, AND YOU WAG IT REALLY WELL! SINCE I DON'T HAVE A TAIL OF MY OWN, MAYBE I COULD BE THE SECOND-BEST PRESENT HERE!"

5

"LEAPIN' LIZARDS!"

NEIGHED RALPHY THE RED ROCKING HORSE. "YA'LL MUST HAVE HAY FOR BRAINS IF YOU THINK A DOGGIE FULL OF STUFFIN' OR A SILLY-LOOKIN' SOCK MONKEY WITH NO TAIL IS BETTER THAN ME!

I CAN ROCK BACK AND FORTH AND BOUNCE UP AND DOWN. AND MY NEW COWBOY SADDLE IS THE BEST IN TOWN! SO, FELLAS, AS YOU CAN PLAINLY SEE, I'M THE GREATEST GIFT UNDER THIS HERE TREE!"

SAMPSON'S HAPPY FACE CHANGED TO A SAD LITTLE SOCK-MONKEY FROWN. "I DON'T HAVE A TAIL LIKE BABY AND I CAN'T BOUNCE UP AND DOWN LIKE RALPHY," THOUGHT SAMPSON. "I GUESS I'M REALLY ONLY THE THIRD-BEST TOY FOR CHRISTMAS."

DIDI THE DANCING DOLL, WHO HAD PRETENDED NOT TO BE LISTENING, SAID,

"YOU ARE ALL AS MISTAKEN AS YOU CAN POSSIBLY BE,

IF YOU THINK A RED HORSE, A BLUE DOG, OR A SILLY-LOOKING SOCK MONKEY IS MORE ADORABLE THAN ME!"

"WITH THE TWIST OF A KEY
I CAN PLAY MY OWN SONG.
YOU CAN HEAR MY SWEET MUSIC
ALL DAY LONG.
JUST LOOK AT ME DANCE
AND TWIRL ON MY TOES.
I HAVE PRETTY RED HAIR
AND A CUTE BUTTON NOSE!"

POOR SAMPSON WAS NOW FILLED WITH DOUBT. HE THOUGHT, "THIS IS TERRIBLE!"

"I DON'T HAVE A TAIL LIKE BABY THE BULLDOG.

I CAN'T BOUNCE UP AND DOWN LIKE RALPHY THE RED ROCKING HORSE.

I CAN'T TWIRL ON MY TOES LIKE DIDI THE DANCING DOLL.

THERE MUST BE SOMETHING THAT SOMEONE WILL LIKE ABOUT ME!"

SAMPSON THEN TOSSED HIS LITTLE SOCK-MONKEY ARMS UP IN THE AIR AND YELLED.

"I'M THE WORST PRESENT HERE! YOU ALL CAN DO SO MANY WONDERFUL THINGS!"

POOR SAMPSON PUT HIS SAD SOCK-MONKEY FACE IN HIS LITTLE SOCK-MONKEY HANDS AND CRIED, "I'M NOT GOOD ENOUGH TO BE A PRESENT. I'M NOT GOOD ENOUGH FOR ANYTHING!"

SUDDENLY, FROM THE VERY TIP TOP OF THE TALL TREE, CAME THE SWEET VOICE OF THE CHRISTMAS TREE ANGEL. "OH, DEAR LITTLE TOYS, I HEAR THE SAME THING EVERY YEAR."

"SOME TOYS SAY THEY ARE THE BIGGEST AND BEST WHILE OTHERS FEEL THEY DON'T EVEN MATTER.

WELL, EACH AND EVERY ONE OF YOU SHOULD FEEL VERY IMPORTANT THIS CHRISTMAS DAY!" SAID THE ANGEL AS SHE FLEW DOWN NEXT TO SAMPSON.

"YOU SEE, CHRISTMAS IS A VERY SPECIAL DAY. THERE IS NO OTHER DAY LIKE IT. ALL OF YOU ARE A PART OF THE WONDERFUL CELEBRATION!" SAID ANGEL.

17

ALL THE TOYS GATHERED AROUND ANGEL AND ASKED, "WHAT ARE WE CELEBRATING? WE THOUGHT THIS WAS JUST A DAY TO GIVE THE BEST TOYS."

"CHRISTMAS IS THE DAY

THE CHRISTMAS STORY

WE CELEBRATE THE BIRTH OF A VERY SPECIAL BABY," SAID ANGEL.

20

"A BABY?

WHAT DOES A BABY HAVE TO DO WITH CHRISTMAS AND TOYS?" BARKED BABY THE BULLDOG.

"WHEN JESUS WAS BORN, PEOPLE CELEBRATED HIS BIRTH BY OFFERING HIM ALL KINDS OF SPECIAL GIFTS.

AND THAT'S WHY GIFTS LIKE ALL OF YOU ARE GIVEN ON CHRISTMAS DAY. IT'S TO CELEBRATE THE PRECIOUS GIFT GOD GAVE!"

PEOPLE CELEBRATED

"SO ALL OF US TOYS ARE GIVEN TO CELEBRATE JESUS' BIRTH?

EVEN A SILLY-LOOKING SOCK MONKEY WITH NO TAIL?"

ASKED SAMPSON, WHO WAS BEGINNING TO FEEL A LITTLE LESS SAD.

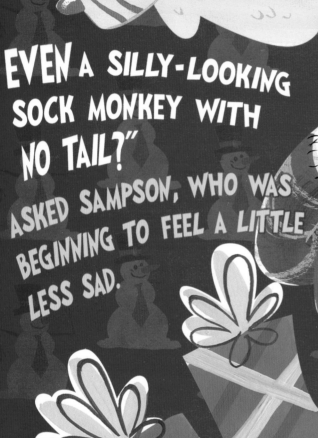

SAMPSON WAS SUDDENLY HIS OLD HAPPY SOCK-MONKEY SELF AGAIN.

HE WAS MORE EXCITED THAN EVER TO CELEBRATE CHRISTMAS. HE REALIZED CHRISTMAS WASN'T ABOUT WAGGING A TAIL, BOUNCING UP AND DOWN, DANCING ON TIPPY TOES, OR EVEN CHUGGING AROUND TRAIN TRACKS.

CHRISTMAS WAS ABOUT CELEBRATING THE BIRTH OF JESUS,

AND THAT MADE SAMPSON ONE VERY HAPPY SOCK MONKEY.

ONCE THE TOYS HEARD THAT CHRISTMAS WAS ABOUT CELEBRATING GOD'S LOVE, SOMETHING WONDERFUL HAPPENED.

THEY STOPPED FIGHTING OVER WHO WAS THE BEST TOY AND WERE FILLED ON THE INSIDE WITH REAL CHRISTMAS SPIRIT.

THEY DECIDED THEY WANTED TO CELEBRATE, TOO. SO BABY, RALPHY, DIDI, AND TIMMY ALL GOT TOGETHER SECRETLY AND DECIDED THEY WOULD GIVE A SPECIAL GIFT TO SAMPSON.

BABY THE BULLDOG GAVE SOME OF HIS STUFFING.

DIDI THE DANCING DOLL GAVE ONE OF HER SOCKS.

RALPHY THE RED ROCKING HORSE PLUCKED A LONG HAIR FROM HIS MANE, AND

TIMMY THE CHOO-CHOO TRAIN GAVE ONE OF HIS WHEELS.

ALL THE TOYS WORKED TOGETHER AND MADE SAMPSON THE SILLY-LOOKING SOCK MONKEY A REAL SOCK-MONKEY **TAIL!**

SAMPSON WAS SO SURPRISED.

HE HAD NEVER HEARD OF A TOY GETTING A GIFT FOR CHRISTMAS!

HE LOVED HIS NEW TAIL, AND IT FIT HIM JUST RIGHT!

AS THE SUN BEGAN TO RISE, ANGEL AND ALL THE TOYS TOOK THEIR PLACES AROUND THE CHRISTMAS TREE. THE TOYS WERE FILLED WITH JOY AND EXCITEMENT BECAUSE NOW THEY KNEW THAT CHRISTMAS WAS REALLY ABOUT THE GIFT OF GOD'S LOVE. AND NO ONE WAS HAPPIER THAN SAMPSON, THE SILLY-LOOKING SOCK MONKEY WITH ONE EAR LARGER THAN THAN THE OTHER AND A BRAND-NEW TAIL!

THE END